First American edition published in 1991 by

Crocodile Books, USA
An imprint of Interlink Publishing Group, Inc.
99 Seventh Avenue • Brooklyn, New York 11215

Originally published in German as *Ein Märchen im Schnee*
by Mangold Verlag, Austria 1990

Library of Congress Cataloging-in-Publication Data available
Card Catalog # LC 90-2545

ISBN 0-940793-67-9

Printed and bound in Hong Kong

THE
WOODCUTTER'S
MITTEN

An Old Tale Retold and Illustrated
by Loek Koopmans

Crocodile Books, USA

An imprint of Interlink Publishing Group, Inc.
NEW YORK

One cold winter morning, a woodcutter and his little dog went for a walk in the forest. They were walking along side by side when the old man dropped his mitten. There it lay on the frozen ground.

Soon afterwards, a cold little mouse came along.
"This is a perfect home for me!" she squeaked.

A little later, a frog stopped in front of the mitten.
"Who lives in this mitten?" he asked.
"My name is Mistress Mouse. And who are you?"

"I am Frog Limpyleg. May I come in?"
"Sure, come on in."
So Frog Limpyleg moved into the mitten with Mistress Mouse
and they were very comfortable.

After a while, a rabbit arrived.
"Who lives in this mitten?" he asked.
"I am Mistress Mouse and this is Frog Limpyleg.
And who are you?"

"I am Rabbit Fast-on-Foot and I would love to live with you
in your mitten."
"Sure, come on in."

Then came a little fox. She also asked: "Who lives here?"
"Mistress Mouse, Frog Limpyleg and Rabbit Fast-on-Foot."
"And I am Fox Goldenfur. May I come in?"

"Sure, come on in."
And the four of them snuggled into the mitten and they were very warm and cozy.

Then a boar came. "Who lives here?" he grunted.
"Mistress Mouse, Frog Limpyleg, Rabbit Fast-on-Foot and
Fox Goldenfur. And who are you?" said the other animals.

"I am Boar Flatnose and I also
want to live here," he snorted.
"Oh no! You are too fat," the other
animals shouted.
But they felt sorry for him so they said: "Let's see If we cuddle together, maybe we
can fit you in."

They somehow managed to squeeze the boar into the mitten. And
there they were, all five animals, cuddled very close together
in their new home.

Suddenly, they heard some branches cracking. . .and a deep growly
voice said: "Who lives in this mitten?"

"Mistress Mouse,
Frog Limpyleg,
Rabbit Fast-on-Foot,
Fox Goldenfur and
Boar Flatnose.
And who are you?"
"Growl. . . .Growl. . . .I am called Master Bigfoot.
Let me in!"
"But there is no room any more!"
"There must be!" said the bear.

"Make yourselves as small as possible."
And would you believe it? That big bear also fit into the mitten!

Meanwhile, on the other side of the forest,
the old woodcutter suddenly noticed that he had lost his mitten.

He turned around and went straight back to look for it.

At last, the little dog found the mitten. But what was that?
It moved as if it were alive!

"Woof, woof, woof!" the little dog barked.
The six animals were so startled, they all jumped out of the mitten
and ran off into the forest.

The old woodcutter arrived, picked up his mitten and patted his dog.
"Good doggy," he said.